Traction Man
meets
Turbodog
MINI GREY

SPECIAL OFFER
FREE (ish) TURBODOG ™
JUST COLLECT 32 TURBO-COUPONS AND WE'LL SEND YOU A FULLY-OPERATIONAL TURBODOG (BATTERIES NOT INC...
Send your 32 coupons with an SAE and a postal o... to cover pos...

NEW TURBODOG ™
STOP INTRUDER!
...AN'S ...L ...NION ...LY HYGIENIC WIPE-CLEAN SURFACE

PLASTIC BATTERIES

AN ACCESSORY IN TOY...

JONATHAN CAPE
London

...and PLEASE stay out of the mud today.

Traction Man is here!
(And his faithful pet Scrubbing Brush too!)

The only way back is through the swampy marshes of the Pond.

They can cross by Boot.

Traction Man and Scrubbing Brush are drying off in front of the heater.

Traction Man is wearing a knotted spotted hanky.

Scrubbing Brush is encrusted with dried-on dirt.

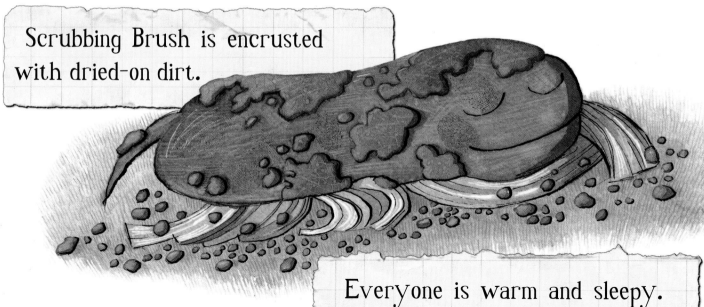

Everyone is warm and sleepy.

Traction Man and Turbodog are crossing the wastes of the Sandpit.

Somewhere under the shifting sands are the ruins of the Handbag.

Maybe that's a corner of it there. The Handbag Dwellers are very shy.

Traction Man and Turbodog are watching Turbodog's greatest adventures on TV.

STOP INTRUDER!

Turbodog thinks it is just getting to the good bit.
This is what Turbodog likes to do BEST.

Scrubbing Brush!
I must find my brave pet!
Where can Scrubbing Brush be?

Traction Man is searching in their favourite hiding places.

The toy cupboard . . .

He wears his Airtight Astro-Suit with Glass Head-Globe.
The atmosphere at the Bin's surface may be deadly poisonous.

Traction Man takes a bottle of **SuperStrong GERMO** (with Ammonia).

No one has ever returned alive from the Bin before.

Traction Man and Scrubbing Brush are going free-diving in the Steaming Tropical Waters of the Tub. Turbodog has come too.

I WILL BE YOUR PET

Traction Man is wearing his Elasticated Micro-Suit, Shark Knife and Slimline Snorkel.

Turbodog is floating on the SS Sponge.

Scrubbing Brush is looking much cleaner.

There's a fizz and a flicker.

Oh dear.

Traction Man and Scrubbing Brush are
Surviving for the afternoon in the
shrubbery near the Pond.
Traction Man has his Magnetic Compass,
First Aid Kit and Survival Vest.
They have constructed a shelter from
pillow cases and a bath mat.

The Dollies are looking after Turbodog.
He is very quiet now (they had to
take out his rusty batteries).

Scrubbing Brush is wearing a
Badge of Cleanness
and has been foraging for Supplies.
Traction Man is helping
Scrubbing Brush to stay clean.
And of course, they are both
Prepared for
Anything.

This book is dedicated to Ian Craig

TRACTION MAN MEETS TURBODOG
A JONATHAN CAPE BOOK 978 0 224 07048 5

Published in Great Britain by Jonathan Cape,
an imprint of Random House Children's Books
A Random House Group Company

This edition published 2008

1 3 5 7 9 10 8 6 4 2

RANDOM HOUSE CHILDREN'S BOOKS
61-63 Uxbridge Road, London W5 5SA

www.kidsatrandomhouse.co.uk
www.rbooks.co.uk

Addresses for companies within The Random House Group Limited can be found at:
www.randomhouse.co.uk/offices.htm

THE RANDOM HOUSE GROUP Limited Reg. No. 954009

A CIP catalogue record for this book is available from the British Library.

Printed and bound in Malaysia

THE MYSTERIOUS SHROOMS
WOULD LIKE TO THANK
STEVE COLE FOR HIS HELP
WITH THEIR LOAMWORK.